Copyright © 2014 by Mattel, Inc. All rights reserved. MONSTER HIGH and associated trademarks are owned by and used under license from Mattel, Inc.
Cover design by Steve Scott
Cover © 2014 by Mattel, Inc.
Interior design by Kay Petronio

In accordance with the U.S. Copyright Act of 1976, the scanning, uploading, and electronic sharing of any part of this book without the permission of the publisher is unlawful piracy and theft of the author's intellectual property. If you would like to use material from the book (other than for review purposes), prior written permission must be obtained by contacting the publisher at permissions@hbgusa.com. Thank you for your support of the author's rights.

Little, Brown and Company

Hachette Book Group
237 Park Avenue, New York, NY 10017
Visit us at lb-kids.com
monsterhigh.com

Little, Brown and Company is a division of Hachette Book Group, Inc.
The Little, Brown name and logo are trademarks of Hachette Book Group, Inc.

The publisher is not responsible for websites (or their content) that are not owned by the publisher.

First Edition: September 2014

Library of Congress Control Number: 2014933503

ISBN 978-0-316-27709-9

10 9 8 7 6 5 4 3 2 1

CW

Printed in the United States of America

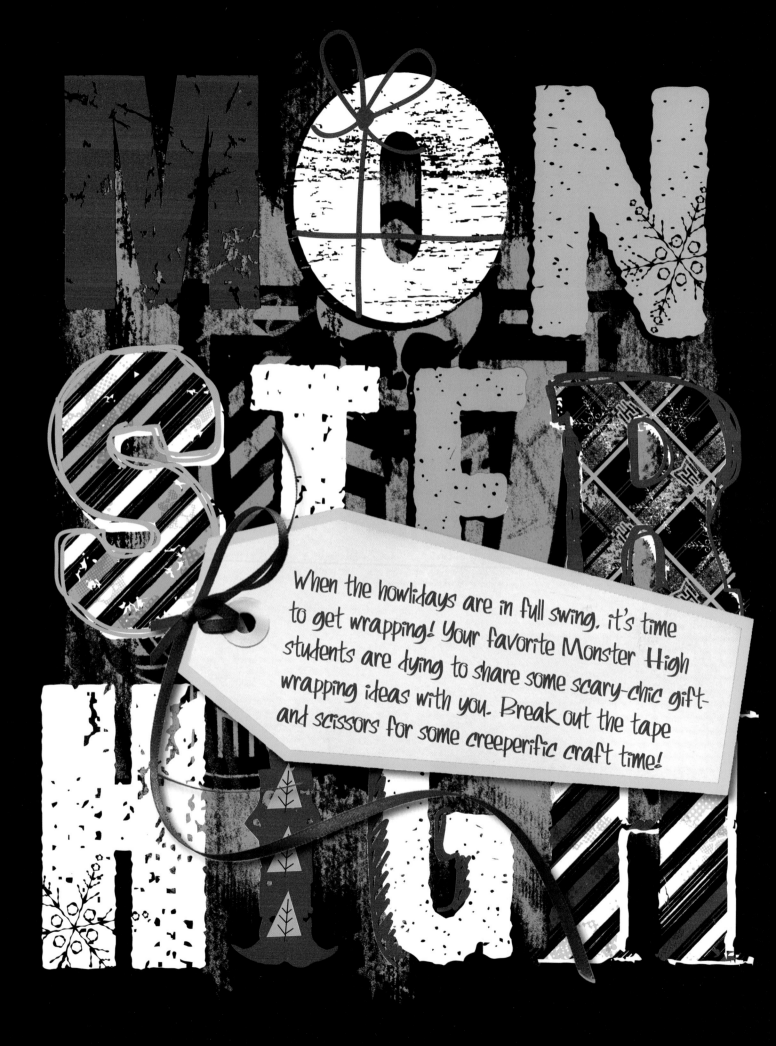

When the howlidays are in full swing, it's time to get wrapping! Your favorite Monster High students are dying to share some scary-chic gift-wrapping ideas with you. Break out the tape and scissors for some creeperific craft time!

TOTALLY VOLTAGE

Howliday presents get me all amped up. I love giving and receiving brand-new things! I got a chic gold chain for Clawdeen—check out my scary-cool plan for wrapping it!

ELECTRIC GIFT WRAP

Use metallic pipe cleaners to create scary-cool shapes around a present to get your ghoulfriend's current going.

INSTRUCTIONS:

1. Wrap the gift in a voltageous paper. I like plaid!

2. Twist the ends of the pipe cleaners into loops and connect them to make a longer cable. Then wrap pipe cleaners around the length and width of the present like a ribbon.

3. Make killer shapes with more pipe cleaners—lightning bolts, neck bolts, Watzits—and hang them off the pipe cleaner "ribbon" like charms.

TOPPER WITH ZAP

This boltrageous gift topper doubles as a creepy-cool keychain.

INSTRUCTIONS:

1. Find some cool nuts and bolts at a hardware store and paint them with glow-in-the-dark paint.

2. Wrap a pipe cleaner around a bolt, or thread it through nuts and knot the ends, to make a charm!

3. Secure the charm to the ribbon of the pipe cleaners wrapped around the present.

HEART IN A BOX

HEART IN A BOX SUPPLIES:

- pink wrapping paper
- tape
- black electrical tape
- tracing paper
- construction paper in three shades of pink
- glue
- pencil
- scissors

DRACULAURA

During the howlidays, my family celebrates with a yummy Bitealian feast. (Vegetarian for me, of course!) I'm wrapping a sweet pair of cable earrings for Frankie in pink and black, the colors of caring and scaring!

A BITE OF LOVE

Make your own scary-sweet pink paper covered in hearts—and fangs.

INSTRUCTIONS

1. Wrap your present in pink wrapping paper, then add scary-sweet stripes with black electrical tape.

2. Draw the heart and fangs on the right on tracing paper.

3. Cut out the shapes and use them as stencils to draw hearts and fangs on pink construction paper. Cut them out.

4. Glue the shapes onto your presents.

HEART ♥ EXPLOSION TOPPER

Top your gift with a fangtastic cluster of 3-D hearts!

INSTRUCTIONS

1. Fold a sheet of construction paper (any color) in half. Then draw half of a heart on it, using the folded edge as the center line.

2. Cut out your heart half and unfold the paper.

3. At the indentation of the heart (where the two "hills" meet), draw a short vertical line about one inch or less (depending on the size of your heart) and cut along that line to make two flaps.

4. Pull the flaps down so the heart puffs out and glue them together.

5. Repeat to make hearts of different sizes. Glue a cluster of them to the top of your present.

UNDER THE SEA-SON'S GREETINGS

- computer paper (or similar)
- tape
- white crayon
- watercolor paints
- water
- paintbrush
- green and blue ribbon
- scissors
- glue
- sequins

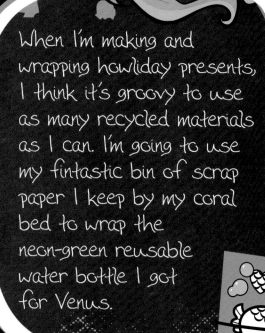

LAGOONA

When I'm making and wrapping howliday presents, I think it's groovy to use as many recycled materials as I can. I'm going to use my fintastic bin of scrap paper I keep by my coral bed to wrap the neon-green reusable water bottle I got for Venus.

TRUE-BLUE GIFT WRAP

Create your own freaky-chic underwater wrapping paper with crayons and watercolors.

INSTRUCTIONS:

1. Lay out enough sheets of paper to cover your present and tape the sheets together along their edges. (The side with tape will be the underside.)

2. Draw boo-tiful underwater patterns— fish, mermaids, waves, sea plants—all over your paper with the white crayon.

3. Paint your paper with seaworthy watercolors. (The crayon drawings will reveal themselves as you paint!) Once the paper is dry, you can wrap your present.

SCARY SEAWEED TOPPER

Make a trailing bow that doubles as a blooming hair ribbon, mate!

INSTRUCTIONS:

1. Cut strands of green and blue ribbon in different lengths, from six to eighteen inches. Cut some strands four inches long and set aside.

2. Braid or twist some of the pieces together; leave others as single strands. Use four-inch strands to tie some other pieces into bunches.

3. Use long pieces of ribbon to tie your braids, twists, strands, and bunches together into a big, flowing burst of seaweed. Glue sequins on the seaweed, then attach it to the top of your present with some ribbon.

GOLDEN GIFT

GOLD AND GAUZE

With gold paper and gauze ribbon, wrap a present that's fit for a queen.

INSTRUCTIONS

1. Wrap your present in gold wrapping paper.

2. Glue metal studs on the top and sides of your present, either at random or in a freaky-fab pattern.

3. Wrap the gauze ribbon around the present both widthwise and lengthwise. Glue studs to the gauze for extra pizzazz.

Wrapping howliday presents is my second-favorite thing about the howlidays! My favorite thing is _unwrapping_ howliday presents, obvi.

Check out this royal gift wrap. I'm going to use it for the scary red nail polish I'm giving to Ghoulia.

AMULETS ON TOP

Using metallic beads and pipe cleaners, create your own chic amulets to top everything off. Your ghoulfriend will look like a queen if she uses these as necklace pendants!

INSTRUCTIONS:

1. String several beads onto a pipe cleaner and make a monstrously fabulous shape with the pipe cleaner.

2. Repeat step one until you have several amulets, then use additional pipe cleaners to attach the amulets to the gauze ribbon on the present.

3. Experiment with more types of amulets! Try using different numbers of beads, making different pipe-cleaner shapes, or making *really* different shapes by using different patterns of beads on one or both ends of the pipe cleaners. Totally royal.

FURRIFIC FUN

SEVENTEEN

FOURTEEN

FURRIFIC FUN SUPPLIES:

- newspaper
- tape
- pink and black markers
- spool of purple ribbon (at least 12 yards)
- scissors
- safety pins

WILD WRAPPINGS

DIY leopard-print paper will make your ghoulfriend go wild!

INSTRUCTIONS:

1. Tape sheets of newspaper together to create the base of the wrapping paper for your present.

2. Go animal-print by using your pink marker to draw uneven leopard spots of different sizes all over the paper, then partially outlining each blob with your black marker.

3. Use tape to wrap the present with your leopard-print paper.

With a whole pack to play with, the beast part of the howliday season is my family's killer annual fur-ball fight! Giving presents is pretty claw-some too. Look at the fierce wrapping job I'm going to do for the fashion sketchbook I got for Jinafire!

PAWFECT PURPLE

Give the leopard print a stylin' leash with this braided purple bow. Your ghoulfriend can attach it to her book bag for a chic look!

INSTRUCTIONS:

1. Wrap purple ribbon around the present widthwise and lengthwise.

2. Cut three pieces of ribbon, each twelve inches long. Tape one end of the ribbons to a stationary surface, then braid them together. Repeat until you have at least six braids.

3. Attach all six braids together by threading one end of each of the braids onto a single safety pin, then thread the other ends onto a second safety pin. Now you have a single rope of braids.

4. Fold the two ends into the center of the braid so that you have two loops, and use a third safety pin to hold them in place.

5. Decorate the bow with more safety pins, then use ribbon to tie the explosion of braids onto the top of the present.

DEAD FAST WRAPPING

DEAD FAST WRAPPING
SUPPLIES:

- ★ newspaper
- ★ tape
- ★ computer paper
- ★ markers
- ★ scissors
- ★ glue

Every yuletide, the Yelps family gathers together to watch *It's a Wonderful Unlife.* Frankie will love the comic books I bought her, because she loves trying new things. And I'm wrapping them in zombie comic-themed paper!

SPEECHLESS PAPER

Make dead-clever wrapping paper out of oversize speech balloons. Then you can fill some of them with inside jokes with your ghoulfriend!

INSTRUCTIONS:

1. After putting your present in a box, wrap it in newspaper.

2. On the computer paper and newspaper, draw a bunch of speech balloons like the one above. Outline them in thick marker, then cut them out.

3. Glue the speech balloons all over the wrapped present so the newspaper is completely covered.

4. Tear some strips of newspaper and glue them to the edges and corners of the present for a chic, ragged look.

5. Now write messages to your ghoulfriend in some of the balloons!

EXPLOSION ON TOP

Give your prezzie comic-book pizzazz with pop-up sound-effects bursts.

INSTRUCTIONS:

1. On the computer paper, draw three bursts like the one above. Outline them in thick marker, then cut them out.

2. Write a sound-effect word (like *Kapow!*, *Bam!*, or *Zap!*) on each burst.

3. Cut three strips of computer paper one inch wide and four inches long. Fold them accordion-style three times (to make four sections). Now you have three springs.

4. Glue one end of a spring to one of your bursts and the other end to the top of your present. Repeat with your remaining springs and bursts.

SNAKES ON A PRESENT

SNAKES ON A PRESENT SUPPLIES:
- paper
- tape
- ruler
- pencil
- colored pencils
- green pipe cleaners
- googly eyes
- glue

DEUCE

GIVING YOUR GHOULFRIEND A PRESENT AT THE HOWLIDAYS IS ALWAYS A GOOD IDEA, WHICH IS WHY I'M USING THIS HISSFUL SNAKE WRAPPING JOB TO GIVE CLEO A CLAW-SOME TURQUOISE BRACELET.

KILLER KICKS

Make cool checkered paper that looks like Deuce's sneaks.

INSTRUCTIONS:

1. After putting your present in a box, lay out enough sheets of paper to cover your present, and tape the sheets together along the edges. (The side with tape will be the underside.)

2. Use the ruler and pencil to draw vertical lines down the length of the paper, keeping one inch between each of the lines. Then draw horizontal lines across the paper, also keeping one inch between each line. You should have a grid of one-inch squares.

3. Color a checkered pattern onto the grid using the colored pencils.

4. Draw the Monster High skullette on some of the squares, then wrap the present in your killer new paper.

CAN OF SNAKES

Top your present with a do as fangtastic as Deuce's—a bunch of homemade snakes! Your ghoulfriend can keep them as scary-cool pets.

INSTRUCTIONS:

1. Twist several pipe cleaners together to make a thick snake that's about six inches long from nose to tail, then shape a head at one end and a tail at the other. Glue two googly eyes to the head.

2. Repeat step one until you have six snakes.

3. Use additional pipe cleaners and tape to attach the snakes to the top of your present.

ROBOT WRAPPINGS

I get a kick out of spending the howlidays rocketing around the ice-skating rink. It's a creeperific change from the Skultimate Roller Maze!

I set myself a reminder so I wouldn't forget to wrap Rochelle's day planner using this steamerific wrapping project!

ALL DUCT OUT

Use some duct tape to piece together your own patchwork of metallic wrapping paper.

INSTRUCTIONS:

1. Place your gift in the gift box. Wrap it in metallic paper.

2. Decorate the box with stripes and patterns of duct tape to create a shiny metallic patchwork.

PENNY FOR YOUR THOUGHTS

Crown your present with a 3-D replica of Captain Penny. She'll look like the cat's pajamas!

INSTRUCTIONS:

1. Using tracing paper and pencil, trace this drawing of Penny, cut out the tracing, and use it as a stencil to draw two images of Penny on the poster board.

2. Cut out the Penny shapes and paint them copper.

3. When the penguins are completely dry, bend their feet forward. Then, except for the feet, glue their backs together. Set aside to dry.

4. Use a ruler to draw a two-inch square on the poster board. Cut out the square and paint it copper.

5. When the square and penguin are dry, glue the penguin's feet to the square. When that's dry, tape the square to the top of your present.

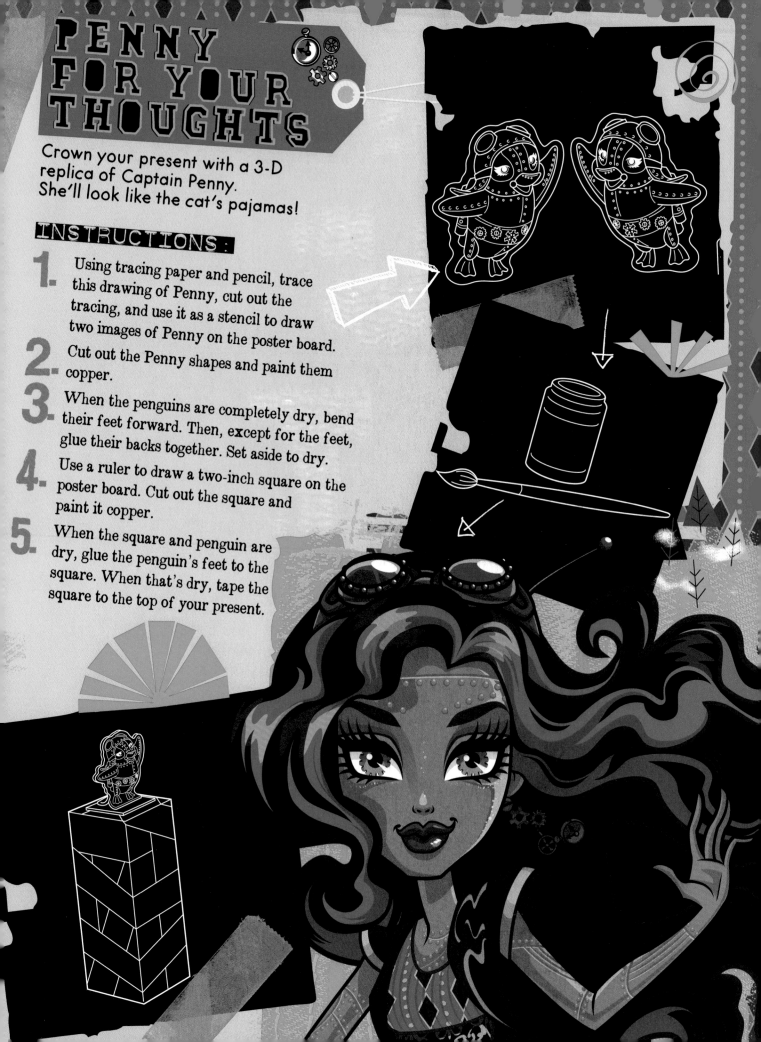

NATURAL WRAPS

VENUS

NATURAL WRAPS SUPPLIES:

NATURAL WRAPS SUPPLIES:
- leaves
- pen or marker
- old newspapers and magazines
- scissors
- glue
- 3 large pinecones
- neon pink and neon green acrylic paints
- paintbrush
- glue gun
- green ribbon (long enough to tie around present)

The McFlytraps gather at the howlidays for a scary sing-along by glow-in-the-dark candlefright (it's better for the planet than using electricity). My favorite tune is "Frosty the Glowman."

I'm using this creeptacular natural wrapping project for the spooky-sweet heart-shaped vegan cookies I baked for Draculaura.

LEAF WRAP

Go jump in a pile of leaves—then gather them up to help make some naturally spooktacular paper.

INSTRUCTIONS:

1. Gather a few fresh leaves of different shapes and sizes and use them as stencils to draw leaf shapes on colorful magazine pages with a pen or marker.

2. Cut out your magazine leaves and glue them in a claw-some pattern on the newspaper.

3. When the glue is dry, wrap a present in your new leaftastic paper.

POLLENTASTIC PINECONES

Top off your luscious leaves with some attention-grabbing neon pink and neon green pinecones.

INSTRUCTIONS:

1. Gather three large pinecones and paint them neon pink and neon green. You can try out different patterns: every other scale a different color, each pinecone its own color, vertical stripes, horizontal stripes—let your imagination go wild!

2. After the pinecones dry, ask an adult to help you attach them to a piece of ribbon using the glue gun, then tie the ribbon around your present. They'll look scary-chic hanging from your ghoulfriend's mirror!

PRESENT PARFAIT

BOO-LA-LA

Use the Frightful Tower to make haunt couture Scarisian wrapping paper fit for Jean Maul Ghostier.

INSTRUCTIONS:

1. After putting your present in a box, lay out enough sheets of pink and teal construction paper to cover the box.

2. Tape the sheets together along the edges. (The side with tape will be the underside.)

3. Use a pencil to trace the Frightful Tower onto tracing paper, then cut it out to use as a stencil.

4. Draw images of the Frightful Tower all over your wrapping paper, then use pink and teal glitter pens to decorate them. Use tape to wrap the present.

According to paragraph 16.4 of the Gargoyle Code of Ethics, c'est très important, it's very important, to wrap your gifts with care. Try using my gift-wrapping ideas below. I am using them for the copper pocket watch I am giving Robecca.

ROT-IRON CUFF TOPPER

A chic cuff bracelet adds Scarisian flair—and is a bonus *cadeau*, present, for your ghoulfriend.

INSTRUCTIONS

1. Wrap a pipe cleaner around your wrist in a **C** shape with the ends each sticking out about an inch. Bend the ends toward your elbow ninety degrees.

2. Repeat with a second pipe cleaner, but this time, bend the end pieces toward your fingers.

3. Set the two **C** shapes next to each other and twist their bent ends together to make a 3-D **C** shape. This is the base of your cuff.

4. Use more pipe cleaners to create a chic design on your cuff by twisting them around the base in different patterns. Short pipe cleaners can make stripes, and long ones can make zigzags or other designs.

UP IN FLAMES

IT'S A FIRE

UP IN FLAMES SUPPLIES:

UP IN FLAMES SUPPLIES:
- orange, yellow, and red tissue paper
- tape
- gold ribbon
- scissors
- twist tie
- stapler
- glue gun
- barrette
- ribbon

Whenever I am having difficulty thinking of the perfect present for a ghoulfriend, I light the fires of creativity by doodling or writing in my journal and seeing what comes to mind. I made a beautiful wooden sewing box for Skelita!

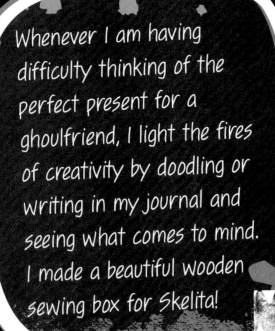

WRAPS ON FIRE

Make some claw-some flaming paper that will burn with howliday cheer!

INSTRUCTIONS:

1. After putting your present in a box, lay out twice as many sheets of orange tissue paper as it will take to cover your present and tape the sheets together along their edges. Do this again with the orange paper, then twice each with red and yellow so that you have two large sheets of each color.

2. Stack the paper together with orange on the bottom, then red, then yellow. Set the box in the middle of the stack and gather all the paper ends up to the top, then tie it with ribbon.

3. Use the scissors to shape the cloud of paper at the top of the gift. Cut single straight lines at staggered spots, then taper some of the ends into flame shapes and crinkle others with your hands.

DARE TO HAIR

Top your present with a homemade hair accessory!

INSTRUCTIONS:

1. Make a stack of six sheets of yellow tissue paper.

2. Fold the stack accordion-style, with each fold about one inch wide.

3. Now fold that in half lengthwise so the ends are together.

4. Lay the twist tie around the fold in the middle. With an equal amount of the twist tie on either side of the tissue paper, securely twist it around the tissue paper several times.

5. Staple the two sides of tissue paper just above the twist tie to hold it in place.

6. Carefully fan out the tissue paper one sheet at a time to make a fangtastic flower shape.

7. With an adult's help, attach the paper flower to the barrette using the glue gun, then use ribbon to tie it around the base of the flames on the present.

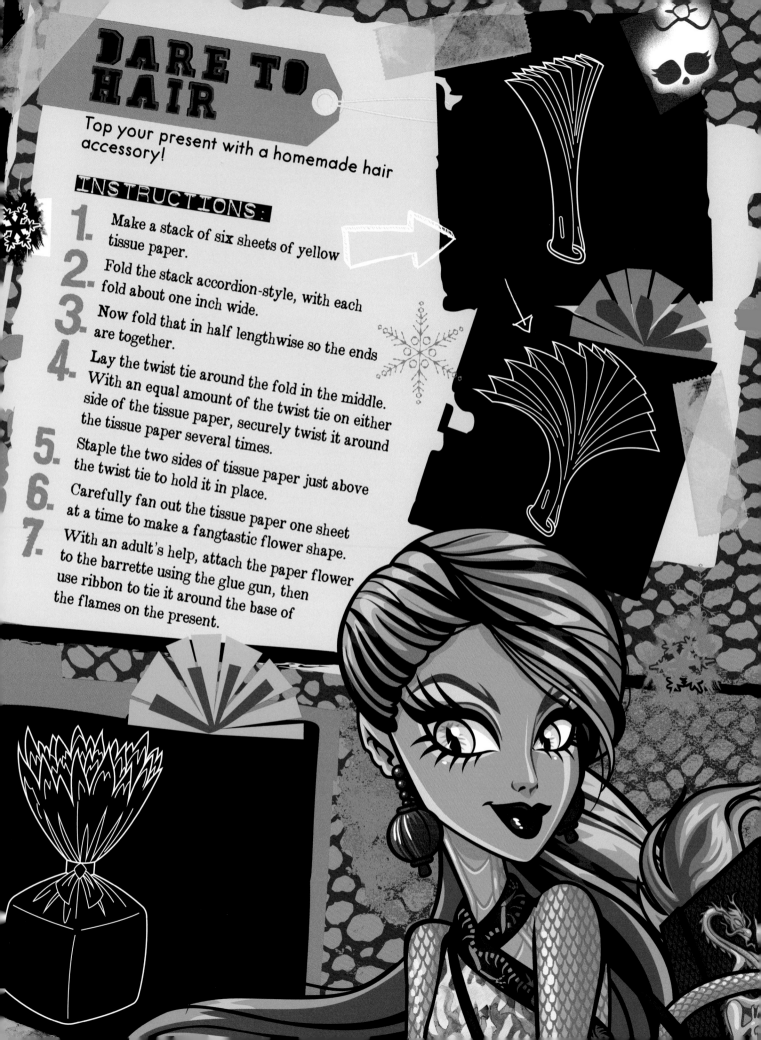

HEXICAN WRAP DRESS

At the howlidays, like many Hexican families, mi familia makes a spookiñata, which we fill with candy, then try to break open. Muy delicioso! I made a bonita skirt for Clawdeen that I'm wrapping in bright colors and bold patterns.

LIVING LACE

Make your own *bonita* patchwork of colorful lace wrapping paper!

INSTRUCTIONS:

1. After putting your present in a box, wrap it in a brightly colored paper.

2. Cut your doilies into boo-nique shapes.

3. Glue the doilies to your gift so that it is completely covered with lace print.

hint: Apply a thin layer of glue with a paintbrush so you don't tear the paper!

BUTTERFLY TOPPER

Make a flock of butterflies on top of your fabulosa gift.

INSTRUCTIONS

1. Tear out a colorful page from a garden magazine and use your pen and ruler to draw a diamond shape that is five inches on each side. Cut out the diamond.

2. Starting at one corner, accordion-fold your diamond all the way across, with folds that are about a quarter-inch wide.

3. Repeat steps one and two with a new diamond that is four inches on each side.

4. Bend a pipe cleaner in half and twist the ends once so there's an open loop below the twist and two pipe cleaner ends above the twist.

5. Squeeze your four-inch diamond in the middle so it looks like a bow (or a pair of wings!) and place it at the point where the two ends of the pipe cleaner meet, with one wing on each side. Then do the same with the five-inch diamond, placing it on top of the four-inch diamond.

6. Twist the pipe cleaner around the diamonds to hold them in place. Curve the pipe cleaner ends to look like antennae, and fan out your butterfly's wings.

7. Make as many butterflies as you like to cover the top of the present, then them on with ribbon.

MONSTER wRAP

Great wrapping job, ghoulfriends! Feel free to hexperiment by adding your own boo-tique twists to each project.

Here are some ideas for some claw-some homemade cards to go with your gifts!

GLOW-WRAP IT UP

Glow-in-the-dark paint will give your card extra electric zing.

FISHY WISHES FROM NEPTUNA

Sandwich plastic wrap between two pieces of construction paper to make a see-through fishbowl card!

CALLIGRAPHY CARD

Use calligraphy to make the beast card your ghoulfriend has ever seen.

"BATTY FOR YOU" CARD

Make a bat-shaped card with a heart inside!

FLEUR-DE-LIS CARD

Decorate a card with a silver glitter fleur-de-lis to look as if it just arrived from Scaris!

SUGAR SKULL CARD

Decorate a sugar skull card for your *ghoulamiga*.

Have a last-minute gift to wrap? Don't worry—these ghoulfriends have it covered! Use the fangtastic stickers and punch-out gift tags on the next two pages to decorate defrightful presents!